GIANNA THE GREAT
By Becky Villareal

Gianna the Great
By Becky Villareal
Copyright © 2015 Becky Villareal

Published by Anaiah Adventures
An imprint of Anaiah Press, LLC

First Anaiah Adventures Print edition March, 2015
ISBN: 978-0-9961297-9-4

This book is dedicated to my mother (my past), to my husband (my present), and to Tatum Rene my proofreader and my future.

Chapter One

I was nosey. That's what everyone said about me.

"Gianna, you always want to get into everybody's stuff!" they'd say.

But it wasn't that. I was just interested in people and why they did things. I couldn't help it if I asked questions in class. Like one time I asked, "What if George Washington didn't *want* to be our first president?" The kids in the class just groaned.

Mary Nichols, who sat beside me, glared at me when I asked that question.

I just wanted to know about things, that's all.

So when Ms. Collins, the social studies teacher, opened an after-school history club, I was the first one to join.

I thought I would have to fight my way in the door at the first meeting, but there were only three other kids there: a shy third grade girl with long braids, a pudgy looking boy with mustard on his shirt, and... *Matthew Jacobs!*

Not him! Matthew Jacobs was the worst. He thought he was so cool because he always got A's. The teachers loved him! He was a total nerd with thick glasses and curly hair. I thought he looked like a chrysanthemum wearing glasses. Ms. Collins rushed in the door and said, "Sit down now, children."

We looked at each other like, *duh*, because we were already sitting in the desks.

"Let's all get acquainted, shall we? I have the talking stick, so I'll go first." The talking stick was decorated with feathers and shiny ribbon. I hadn't seen something so cheesy since Kindergarten. It was supposed to keep us from all talking at the same time. I didn't know how to break it to her, but by the time kids get to fourth grade, they pretty much say whatever they want—stick or no stick.

Ms. Collins gave the talking stick to the mustard boy first, and he mumbled his name as Tony Something-or-other. Before I could ask him to repeat it, he shoved the stick into the hand of the shy third grader. She had barely whispered her name before quickly handing it to me.

"My name is Gianna Saldana," I said clearly, and smiled at everyone in the room.

Matthew frowned at me and grabbed the stick out of my hands.

"My name is Matthew Jacobs, and I'm in the Talented and Gifted class."

Ms. Collins nodded at each of us quickly and put the talking stick away.

Then she pulled out a piece of chart paper—the kind with the sticky back— and stuck it on the whiteboard. It wrinkled a bit, and she ripped it off the wall to stick it down again.

I got a sick feeling in my stomach. Any teacher who cared that much about a wrinkled up piece of paper was *sure* to be bad news.

With a large red marker, she drew a huge question mark in the middle of the page. Then she turned to us with a glint in her eye and asked,

"Why are you here?"

We looked at each other and shrugged.

"Don't you know?" I asked her. The other kids groaned.

Chapter Two

"Of course she knows, dummy," Matthew Jacobs answered.

I felt my face get hot. I knew I was turning the color of *Mamá's* favorite sweater.

Ms. Collins cleared her throat and continued, "In other words, what do you know about history?"

Before anyone even had a *chance* to think, Matthew Jacobs answered.

"History is the study of past events, particularly in human affairs."

I knew he had memorized that definition right out of the dictionary. I gritted my teeth when he said it. He was just showing off again!

"Yes, Matthew," she answered sweetly, giving him a check in the invisible grade book teachers keep in their heads. Like I said, teachers *loved* him! Yuck!

Ms. Collins kept on talking about the history of the United States for a full thirty minutes. I knew it was because I kept checking the clock.

There is nothing wrong with learning about the United States, but I get that every day from my Social Studies teacher, Ms. Weathers.

I wanted to find out about other places. Like Mexico. Didn't Mexico have history, too?

By the end of the meeting I was thinking I should have joined the science club instead. *Mamá* said I was good at science, and I did like to learn about insects.

I was on my way out of the classroom when Ms. Collins stopped me.

"I hope to see you again next week, Gianna! We're going to be learning a lot about history."

I didn't want to hurt her feelings. After all, she couldn't help it if she didn't know anything else except American history.

"Sure," I said, and then walked out the door.

Chapter Three

I couldn't believe the news all over school the next day: Ms. Collins had fallen in the parking lot and broken her leg! I heard she wouldn't be able to do the History Club anymore.

Oh well, I had already decided I didn't want to go to the History Club meetings anyway. That afternoon Principal Martinez announced Mr.

Williams would be taking over the club. That made me change my mind. Mr. Williams must be close to one hundred years old. I figured he was sure to know a lot more history than Ms. Collins.

It turned out I was right.

The next history club meeting I went to, Mr. Williams was sitting behind the desk. He looked busy and barely glanced up at us as we walked in the door.

There weren't as many of us as there were at the first meeting. The boy with the mustard on his shirt and the shy third grader must have decided to drop out of the club, because they were nowhere in sight. That only left Matthew Jacobs and me. *Sheesh.* I could have done without *him*!

"Come on in," Mr. Williams said and waved us in. We sat at a long table he had at the front of the room.

He took his time walking over from his desk, like I bet he did everything in his classroom. From what the other kids said, he was quiet but really smart. I thought he must have been teaching "since Noah was a boy," like I heard Pastor Canales say from time to time.

He sat at the table in front of us and said, "Well, looks like you are the only two coming."

"There were only four of us to begin with," I said before I could catch myself.

Mr. Williams smiled and looked at each of us. I was waiting for the *Why are you here?* question again. He surprised me when he asked, "What do you want to know?"

Matthew Jacobs looked confused, and asked, "You mean, about anything?"

"Sure, why not?" Mr. Williams answered.

Boy oh boy. That left it opened to anything, anything at all!

Before Matthew could say he wanted to learn about Earth's atmosphere or something, I said, "I want to know about my family." The words were out of my mouth before I knew it. I heard Matthew Jacobs sigh.

Mr. Williams looked at me with his bushy eyebrows bunched up together like a fuzzy white caterpillar.

"What would you like to know?" he asked.

"I'd like to know where they came from, and how they got here," I said.

Mr. Williams scratched his head and asked, "Have you ever asked your folks?"

I shook my head.

"My *Mamá* is all I have. She doesn't know anything about our family. I guess they never talked about it much when she was growing up."

"Some families are like that," he said and nodded, "Mine was. But if you work hard enough, you find out what you want to know." Then he turned to Matthew.

"What about you, son? Do you want to find out about *your* family?"

Matthew only shrugged and looked down at the tops of his shoes. I had heard that his mom had left him with his dad when he was three. Maybe he didn't want to know anything about her. By not saying anything, though, he was giving in to what I wanted to learn about.

Mr. Williams stood up and said, "Well, we might as well get started. But to do this, we need to head over to the computer lab."

I saw a spark of hope in Matthew's eyes. I guess he figured he wasn't going to be bored stiff after all.

Chapter Four

When we got to the lab, it was dark, and all the computers were turned off. It seemed kind of creepy.

Mr. Williams flicked on the lights and sat down at the computer closest to the door. "Okay gather round. We're going to have our first lesson on genealogy."

"I thought we were going to learn about our families, not rocks," I said, remembering my science.

Matthew frowned at me, "That's *geology*, sock brain!"

I gave him the stinky eye.

"Yes, that's right, er... What did you say your name was?" Mr. Williams asked.

Matthew cleared his throat, "Matthew. Matthew Jacobs, sir."

"Oh," was all he said, making me think Mathew had just lost a point in Mr. Williams' invisible grade book. "Now, young lady, you said you wanted to find out about your family. Tell me what you know."

I started thinking really hard. "Well, my name is Gianna Saldana and my *Mamá's* name is Lucinda."

I watched as he opened a website with pictures of families in the background. "Okay, do you know when or where your mother was born?"

"Well, I know her birthday is March the eighth, but I don't know what year. She turned thirty on her last birthday."

"Well, let's do some mental math then," he said, and began to work it out.

Matthew shouted out the year before we could.

"No need to shout young man," Mr. Williams said, and smiled. "But you're right, never the less."

Then he typed the information in to the form on the screen.

There must have been a hundred names on the screen, but Mr. Williams scanned them all and said, "Well, here you are!"

Before I knew it, he had pulled up something that looked like a school roster. He pointed to my name and then over a row to my mother's name. "This is from when you were born, and this is your mother's name."

"Wow," was all I could say. To see my name on a website made me feel special. I didn't even know I could find out stuff like that!

"This is called a birth index. I'll print it off for you and you can show it to your mom. Maybe she could tell you a little bit more."

"Thanks," I said, still getting over seeing my name on a computer website.

Chapter Five

"Ay, mija, why do you want to know about our family?" my mother asked me that night. We were sitting in our kitchen, with the faded yellow wallpaper at the same table I had known since I was a baby. One corner of the table still had a mark where I'd hit it with a rattle.

"*Mamá*, I just want to know. I mean, why don't I look more like you?"

Mamá put her hands around my face. I could feel the calluses on them from her long days of cleaning up after people at the hotel.

"Gianna, you are much more beautiful than I ever could be. Don't you know that?"

I shook my head. Everyone knows mothers have to say junk like that.

"But, *Mamá*, your hair is dark brown and smooth. Mine is curly, and sticks up all over the place when it rains! And you have nice straight teeth. Mine are coming in *crooked*!"

Mamá just smiled and shook her head.

"*Ay, mija*," she said, "You just wait until you're grown! You will be a beautiful swan someday."

I remembered the story of the ugly duckling from school. It took a long, long time for that ugly little duck to become a beautiful swan. If I had to wait that long, I was sure going to find out who I was going to look like!

* * *

"Well, Gianna *the Great*," Matthew Jacobs teased the next day, "did you find out you're related to Benjamin Franklin or something?"

"No, I didn't," I answered, thinking about *Mamá's* reaction to my questions.

"What do you mean? Didn't you show her the paper Mr. Williams gave you?"

"I guess I forgot," I said.

"Forgot! Wow, how silly can you *be*? Don't you know how great it would be to find out about your family?"

"Leave me alone, Matthew!" I was just getting ready to let him have it when Mr. Williams walked up.

"Oh, Gianna," he said before I had a chance to get Matthew back, "I found some more records for you."

"Oh, great!" I said, and really meant it. I wanted to know more.

"I tell you what, I can't meet with you today, but why don't you and Matthew come by my room tomorrow after school?"

"Sure!" Matthew answered before I had a chance to ask why *he* was invited.

"Okay, you'd better get on to class now, before the tardy bell rings," Mr. Williams said with a smile, and walked down the hall. He seemed so happy and excited that suddenly he didn't look as old as I thought he was.

Chapter Six

That night, I remembered to show the birth index to *Mamá*. She was stirring a pan with *chorizo* and eggs when I put it in front of her face.

"See, *Mamá*? Here's my name, and here's yours."

She nodded briefly and then gently pushed the paper out of the way, "I'll look at it in a minute *mija*. Let me finish the *comida*."

I sat down with a thump. She didn't seem as interested in all of this as I felt. Why didn't she want to know more about our family?

She placed the plates of steaming *chorizo* down on the table, then began to heat up the tortillas. The smell of the food made my insides ache with hunger. The only things I ate for lunch were yogurt and carrot sticks; nothing else looked good to me.

At last, she sat down. Without a word, she grabbed my hands and we said grace. Every night, we asked God to bless the food and thanked Him for His blessings.

When she finally picked up the paper and looked at it, she said, "Now, tell me what this is again?"

"It's called a birth index. See all the names? In this row, it shows all the names of the babies who were born on the same day I was. The next row shows the mother's names. See, here's yours!"

She looked at the names carefully and nodded.

When my finger moved over to the next row of names, there was one missing. This was the row of father's names, and there was no name on that row for me.

"Hey!" I said, confused and angry. "Where's my father's name?"

"Well, people make mistakes," my *Mamá* answered.

"You mean they forgot to write it down?"

"*Si*, perhaps that's what happened, Gianna. Now, let's eat before our *comida* gets cold."

I was still thinking, *what a joke*, as I tasted my first forkful of the spicy *chorizo* and eggs.

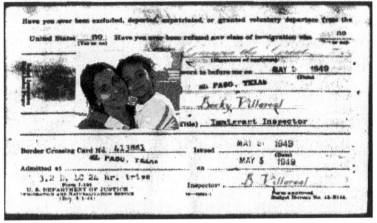

Chapter Seven

The next afternoon, Mr. Williams was waiting at his desk when Matthew and I walked in. He was smiling from ear to ear like a kid with a new pair of Nike's. "Well, there you are. I was wondering if you'd remember to come! Come on in and sit down. I want to show you something!"

Matthew and I walked in and sat down next to him. He had a laptop out and was typing so fast I thought his fingers would fly off.

We scooted up to him as close as we could. He pointed to the information on the screen. "See here?"

Matthew squinted through his glasses, "I see it, but I can't read it. What is that, Mr. Williams?"

He smiled at us both and said, "It's your mother's baptismal records."

"Her *what*?" I asked. I knew some churches baptized people and I had even seen one, but I'd never heard about a record.

Mr. Williams took a deep breath.

"In Mexico," he explained, "when a child is born, the parents and the *padrinos*, the godparents, take the child to church to be baptized by the priest. That is where they receive their full name. Your mother's name is Maria Luisa Del Refugio Padilla Saldana."

"Wow, what a name!" Matthew Jacobs said, and I felt proud that it belonged to my mother.

"That," Mr. Williams said, "is because they receive their mother's maiden name and their father's name at the same time."

"Did you find anything else out?" I wanted to know as much as he could tell me.

"Yes," he said as his fingers flew across the keyboard once again. "I found a border crossing record." What he pulled up next took my breath away. It was a picture of woman and a little girl. The woman looked familiar, but the little girl looked just like me!

I touched the picture on the screen as Mr. Williams told me what it was.

"This is a record of when your mother and *her* mother came to the United States for the first time. It says here that your mother was not much older than you are now. They were coming to visit her aunt, Andrea Saldana, who lived in El Paso."

"Then this is a picture of my grandmother?"

"It sure is," Mr. Williams said with a smile. "I want to show you exactly how I found these records so that you can keep looking on your own."

I wanted to start right then, but I knew *Mamá* would be worried if I didn't get home by a certain time.

"I… I can't, Mr. Williams. But can I get a copy of these papers to show to my mom?"

Mr. Williams shook his head.

"No, I'm sorry. I can't print them off here in the classroom, we would have to go to the computer lab. Why don't we do that tomorrow after school?"

Matthew and I quickly agreed. I could hardly wait to tell *Mamá* about everything I'd found out.

Chapter Eight

I had only been home a little while when *Mamá* walked in the door. She looked tired and a little bit unhappy.

"*Mamá*, you'll never guess what we found!"

Mamá rubbed her back and sat down at the table.

"No, Gianna, not right now."

Holding in all that information was the hardest thing I had ever had to do.

"Are you mad, *Mamá*?" I asked.

She pulled me into her arms, "No, *mija*, I'm not angry. *Yo soy muy cansada*, that's all." I was glad when she said she was just tired. At least I could talk to her later.

Later turned out to be the next morning. She was getting ready for work and needed to walk me to school. All morning she had been rushing around, and I hadn't had the chance to talk to her.

As we walked quickly down the street towards the school, I had to stop to catch my breath.

"*Mamá*! You'll never guess! I saw a picture of your mother!"

Mamá stopped walking and stared at me. "What," she said, "What did you see?"

"A picture of your *mamá*, my *abuelita*."

Mamá shook her head and said, "But you've never even seen her. How would you know what she looked like?"

"I saw a picture of you when you were little. And you were with your *Mamá*!" The words tumbled out of my mouth like jelly beans.

Mamá walked slowly then, listening to every word I said.

"Where did you see this, Gianna?"

"Mr. Williams showed me. You know, my History Club teacher I told you about?"

She nodded, and I could see that she was thinking very hard about what I'd said. Then she began to walk quickly again. She knew that we would be late now if we didn't hurry.

When we got to the front of the school, she grabbed me and held me so tight I thought I wouldn't be able to breathe again for a week.

"*Te amo, mija,*" was all she said before she rushed towards the bus stop.

That night, I showed her the copies of the baptismal records and border crossing. She took them and pressed them to her chest like they were something very precious. Then she began to cry. I'd never seen her cry like that in my whole life.

I put my arms around her as far as they would go.

"It's okay, *Mamá.* It's okay."

Mamá looked at me with her beautiful smile.

"*Está bien,* Gianna. Don't worry! These are happy tears. I want to know more!"

I felt a bubble of joy swell up inside me like I feel when I am at church.

"I can find out more *Mamá*! Lot's more!"

I did, too. But that's for another day...

About the Author

As an elementary teacher and ten year veteran of genealogy, Becky has been able to enjoy not only working with children but find out much more about her family than she ever envisioned.

She also enjoys a good cup of coffee, a quiet place to write, and a warm purring cat on her lap while she types. Go figure.

https://twitter.com/bvillareal
https://www.facebook.com/beckyreadsbooks
http://www.pinterest.com/beckyreadsbooks/
https://vramon249.wordpress.com/

Acknowledgements

I would like to acknowledge all of the indexers who provide hours and hours of work to document genealogical records from all over the world.